FOR MY GRANDCHILDREN, CAROLYN ROSE,
JACOB BOWMAN, AND AVA RAE- AND ALL OF THOSE
IN THE COMING GENERATIONS OF STORYTELLERS
-JB

FOR MY LOVES AT HOME.
NOTHING ELSE MATTERS
-DD

Reycraft Books
55 Fifth Avenue
New York, NY 10003
Reycraftbooks.com

Reycraft Books is a trade imprint and trademark of Newmark Learning, LLC.

Library of Congress Control Number: 2020900901

ISBN: 978-1-4788-6869-9

Author photo courtesy of Eric Jenks
Illustrator photo courtesy of Dale Deforest
Printed in Guangzhou, China
4401/0120/CA22000032
10 9 8 7 6 5 4 3 2 1
First Edition Hardcover published by Reycraft Books

Reycraft Books and Newmark Learning, LLC., support diversity and the
First Amendment, and celebrate the right to read.

REYCRAFT
BOOKS

THE POWWOW DOG

BY JOSEPH BRUCHAC

ILLUSTRATED BY
DALE DEFOREST

1

THE OLD HOUSE

The old house at the edge of the reservation sat empty. It had something like a little house built on top of it.

That's called a cupola, Marie thought.

All the windows were dark. They looked like staring black eyes. The shingles needed paint. The metal roof was rusted. Its front door stood partly open. The only thing nearly new was a garage on the side. The garage door was pulled down.

"That place looks haunted," Marie said.

"It sure does," Jamie agreed.

Grampa slowed down their van to look.

"Nobody there now. Your Grama and I went to Indian School with the man whose family owned that place. Thomas Jefferson Jimmerson. He used to live there."

"Is he . . . you know?" Marie said.

"As far as I know," Grama said, "he's still alive. He moved away about ten years ago. He went to Buffalo to be closer to his grown children. They have good jobs there. Hard to get work around here, you know. We haven't seen Tommy in years."

Jamie turned around in his seat to stare at the house. Did he see something white move next to it? A shiver ran down his back. Then they turned a corner and he lost sight of whatever it was.

"Here we are," Grampa said. A broad field stretched out in front of them. Other vans were already there. Jamie could see people setting up their booths. A fire burned brightly in the center of the dance circle.

2

US INDIANS

By early afternoon, the powwow grounds were crowded with folks of all sorts. Native people and non-natives. African Americans and people who had Spanish accents. Men and women wearing leather jackets and motorcycle boots.

Grampa chuckled.

The twins tried not to stare. But it was so interesting. Some people looked and dressed as if they had come from other countries. They were speaking languages the twins had never heard before.

Grama nodded in the direction of a young woman wearing a colorful sari.

The young woman came to their booth.

I'LL BET SHE'S A STUDENT FROM THE UNIVERSITY. IT'S ONLY THREE MILES FROM HERE.

7

"Hello," she said.

"Kulipaio," Grampa said. "You're welcome here."

The woman beamed a bright smile. "Thank you," she said. "So you are American Indians."

Grama smiled back. "That is what they call us. We just call ourselves people."

"Ah. Well, I am Indian, too. India Indian. I am from Kolkata."

Grama and the young woman began talking about Grama's beaded bracelets.

Before long, the young woman bought three bracelets, including one Marie had made.

THIS ONE IS MY FAVORITE.

OH! DID YOU SEE THAT?

WHOOSH!

The twins looked where the young woman pointed.

Across from them was a stand selling buffalo burgers. THE SENECA CHEF, read the sign. The chef stood behind the table. He had his hands on his hips. His lips were pressed together and he was shaking his head.

The twins looked. The dog was nowhere to be seen. But Marie noticed something she had not seen before. Beyond the far end of the field. It stuck up above the trees. The cupola of the haunted house.

At 2 p.m. the dance competition started. Everyone crowded around the dance circle.

"No customers till the dancing is over," Grama said.

LOOK, WE COULD SEE BETTER THERE.

The twins walked to the edge of the crowd. It was hard to see with so many people around the dance circle.

Off to their right the ground rose up to make a little hill. No one was on it.

But before they reached the hill, four other children climbed on it. Jamie and Marie stopped.

"This is our hill," the biggest kid said. His T-shirt had the design of an eagle on it.

Jamie and Marie started to walk away. "Hey!" the biggest kid said. "Want to join us? I'm Cody."

"And I'm Bear," said the second boy.

"Nicky," said the second girl.

AND THIS IS OUR RESERVATION. THERE'S PLENTY OF ROOM. I'M SUNFLOWER.

Soon all six of them were talking like old friends. It turned out two of the fancy dancers were Cody's brothers. They all watched until the competition was over.

I'D BE OUT THERE BUT I SPRAINED MY ANKLE IN LACROSSE LAST WEEK.

The four kids walked with the twins partway
back to Grama and Grampa's booth. Like the twins,
the four local kids had jobs helping their families at
their booths.

"Which way did you come in?" Cody asked before
they parted. "Off the Interstate onto Frog Street?"

"Unnh-hunnh," Jamie said.

"Did you see Old Man Jimmerson's place?"

The twins nodded.

BUFFALO BURGERS

Marie and Jamie talked over their plan.

"Is your phone charged?" Marie asked. "Good. I'll wait here where I can see the Seneca Chef's booth."

"I'll go way over by those trees."

"And I'll call you if anything happens."

Jamie walked past the hundreds of parked cars to the strip of forest between the powwow grounds and Frog Street and sat down to wait.

Jamie looked up just in time to see a white streak heading straight for him. He had to step aside, or he would have been knocked down by the big dog. It stopped to look back at him. A buffalo burger dangled from its mouth.

Then it turned and ran. It went straight to Old Man Jimmerson's house and through the open door.

He waited until Marie reached him.
The old house looked even spookier now.

Jamie took a deep breath. "Okay," he said, trying to sound as brave as his sister.

They walked over to the old house and paused at the front door.

Marie leaned in. "Hello?" she said, her voice echoing.

A loud WOOF bounced off the walls inside. Jamie grabbed his sister's hand. Then they heard a weak voice. "Help. I'm in here."

They tiptoed inside. An old Native man lay on the floor at the bottom of the stairs. The white dog crouched next to him, wagging its tail.

"Thank the Lord," the old man said. "Been here since I fell down the stairs last night."

Three buffalo burgers sat on the floor next to him. One of them was half-eaten.

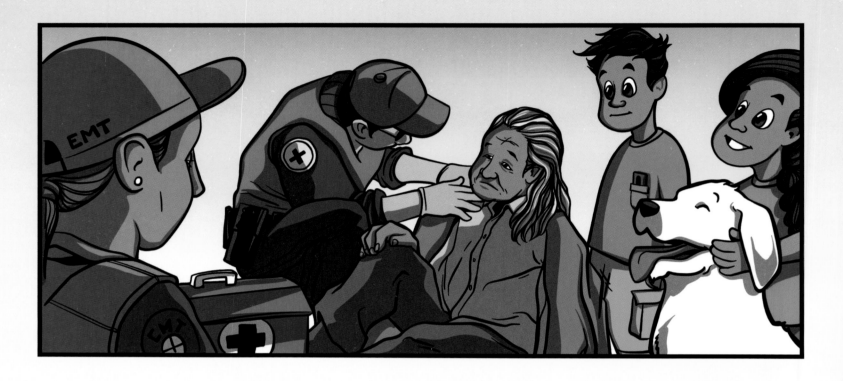

The twins stayed with Mr. Jimmerson until the Emergency Squad arrived.

"You kids did well," one of the Emergency Squad men said to them. "Who knows how long he might have been stuck here. I guess no one saw him come in late last night. Because he put his car in the garage and shut the door, it looked like the place was still empty."

"Is he going to be all right?" Marie asked.

"Can't say for sure. But his vitals are good. I'm guessing a broken hip."

"Children," Mr. Jimmerson waved at them from the stretcher.

"Go ahead," the Emergency Squad man said.

"I guess you saved my life," Mr. Jimmerson said. "Niaweh. Thank you."

Marie shook her head. "It was your powwow dog." She patted the head of the big white dog leaning against her.

"You said you're at the powwow with your grandparents, the Longbows?"

Jamie nodded.

"So you're the grandkids of my old school friends, Bunny and Flash."

Marie looked shocked. Mr. Jimmerson smiled. "That's what everyone called them back then. Will you say hello for me?"

"Of course," said Marie.

"One more thing. Can you take care of Wolfie till my kids can come get him later today? I can see he likes you."

Jamie and Marie both nodded.

"Good. Leash is there by the door. Here."

He reached into his pocket and pulled out a twenty-dollar bill.

Jamie shook his head. "You don't have to pay us."

Mr. Jimmerson laughed and then made a face. The laughing hurt his hip.

"Nope," he said. "But somebody's got to pay for those buffalo burgers."

Meet
JOSEPH BRUCHAC

I'm a writer and traditional storyteller. An enrolled member of the Nulhegan Band of the Abenaki Nation, I've performed as a storyteller and sold books and my own crafts at northeastern powwows since the early 1980s. My family and I run the annual Saratoga Native American Festival at the National Museum of Dance in Saratoga Springs, New York. One of my favorite powwow memories is when I was honored with a blanket at the Shelburne Museum powwow in Vermont twenty years ago.

Meet
DALE DEFOREST

I was born in Tuba City, Arizona, but raised on the Navajo Reservation in northwestern New Mexico. My mother says I've been an illustrator since I was able to hold a crayon. I used to lie on my back and draw pictures under the coffee table in my parents' living room. Apart from being an illustrator, I'm a storyteller, graphic designer, and musician. I reside in Albuquerque, New Mexico, and am a happily married father of two. Anything and everything I do, I do for my loved ones. The ultimate goal of my career is to do what I do, from the comfort of my home. Several of the characters depicted in this adorable story were inspired by loved ones in my own life, namely my mother, sister, and brother.